BACK ROW
DYNAMO

BY JAKE MADDOX

text by
Leigh McDonald

STONE ARCH BOOKS
a capstone imprint

Jake Maddox JV Girls books are published by
Stone Arch Books
a Capstone imprint
1710 Roe Crest Drive
North Mankato, Minnesota 56003

www.mycapstone.com

Library of Congress Cataloging-in-Publication Data is available on the Library of Congress website.

ISBN: 978-1-4965-4926-6 (library binding)
ISBN: 978-1-4965-4928-0 (paperback)
ISBN: 978-1-4965-4930-3 (eBook PDF)

Summary:
Ellie is amazing in the back row but not so good in the front row. When Ellie meets some younger girls in need of volleyball instruction, she sees improvement from a different angle. Will this help Ellie find a way to be a more well-rounded player and not just a back row dynamo?

Art Director: Russell Griesmer
Designer: Kayla Rossow
Media Researcher: Wanda Winch
Production Specialist: Tori Abraham

Photo Credits:
Shutterstock: Aptyp_koK, cover (ball), cluckva, 90-95 (background), Eky Studio, throughout (stripes design), Lightspring, back cover, chapter openers (background, ball), monbibi, chapter openers (background, floor), Trong Nguyen, cover (background), Val Thoermer, cover (player)

Printed and bound in Canada.
010382F17

TABLE OF CONTENTS

FIRST PRACTICE

Ellie's sneakers squeaked loudly on the floor of the empty gym. A big grin spread across her face. She was very excited to get started on the first volleyball practice of the season and had practically flown out of eighth-period math when the bell rang. Sure enough, she was the first team member to arrive.

Two large poles had been bolted into special ports in the gym floor. Coach Henderson was busy hooking a large net to one side.

"Hey, Ellie!" shouted Coach Henderson from a ladder. "Help me get this net up!"

Ellie dropped her gym bag on the bleachers and jogged over to grab the other end of the net. As they worked to raise it up, the gym began to echo with happy voices as the rest of the team streamed in.

Six of the girls on this year's team were veteran players. The other six were new. Ellie and her best friend, Isabella, had played together on the team for two years now. They had been talking all weekend about how excited they were to get started on a third season.

Isabella came running over as Ellie was tying off the last strap on the net. Coach Henderson was tossing volleyballs out of the closet. "Finally!" she said, throwing an arm around Ellie. "I thought this day would never come."

Just then, the coach's whistle echoed through the room. Chatter stopped as everyone faced her.

"Welcome to the Cheetahs, everyone!" Coach Henderson announced, beckoning them closer.

"We have a great team this year, and I think we're going to have a lot of fun!"

Ellie and a few of the others let out a whoop.

"First, I want to welcome any of our brand new team members," the coach continued. "We're really excited to have you joining us this season, and I know the returning Cheetahs will be happy to help you settle in." She gave them an encouraging smile.

Ellie turned to the new girl standing nearest to her, Ally Johnson, and smiled too. Ally was in her English class. She always had great answers for the teacher. *I hope she isn't quite as much of a star on the volleyball court,* Ellie thought, feeling a little bit of worry creeping in. She liked Ally, but the volleyball court was Ellie's place to shine.

"But," Coach Henderson went on, "whether you've been here before or you're new, I want you to remember that we're all learning. Every single one of us is going to make mistakes. That's how we improve, right? As we work together through the season, we're going to grow to be the best players and teammates we can be. But enough talk. Let's play!"

Everyone cheered. Then Coach Henderson had the team spread out on the court. The first warm up was a shuffle passing drill.

"Now, as you have probably noticed," said Coach Henderson, "volleyball players are rarely standing still. It's extremely important to be able to move quickly and change positions in an instant."

Ellie shifted on her feet as she listened, imagining the game. She was getting impatient with the warm-up speech and itching to play.

"Developing a good shuffle is a key foundation for any player. It's great exercise, too. Isabella, would you please come up here by me and show us proper shuffling form?" Coach Henderson asked.

Isabella jogged up to the front of the team and assumed a ready stance. Her feet were shoulder-width apart, knees and arms slightly bent and out in front.

Coach Henderson nodded, and Isabella took a large sideways step with her right foot and then slid her left foot over to match it. She repeated this for a few steps and then shuffled back to her starting point, maintaining the ready stance.

"Thank you, Isabella," Coach Henderson said. "See how she kept her limbs loose but her core engaged? And her feet never crossed each other."

The girls nodded. Isabella ran back into the group and took her spot next to Ellie.

"Okay, make sure you're all at least an arm's length apart," Coach Henderson said.

Ellie reached out and poked Isabella, laughing, before scooting away into her own space.

"Now, assume your ready stance," Coach Henderson said, demonstrating her own.

"When I point, you shuffle in that direction until I point somewhere else. Stay alert, or you might crash into your teammates."

The girls bent their knees and began shuffling quickly back and forth on the court at the coach's direction. Some of the new team members looked a little awkward. Ellie smiled at the familiar feeling. She was right back in volleyball mode.

After a few minutes of shuffling, they finished warming up with dynamic stretches, like twisting lunges and high kicks. Ellie always felt a little silly stomping around the gym like a toy soldier, but Coach Henderson said it was important to stretch and get your muscles moving at the same time.

Finally, they began to work on sets. Coach Henderson called Ellie up to the front this time to demonstrate correct position.

Ellie spread her fingers wide on each hand. She matched them together, thumb to thumb, index finger to index finger, and so on. Then she raised her arms above her head with her elbows out. She moved her hands apart just wide enough for a ball to fit between them.

"Great," Coach Henderson said, turning to the team. "Now, your fingertips are the only part of your body that should contact the ball during a set. I'm going to toss the ball to Ellie, and she will catch it briefly, then push it back to me with a setting motion."

Coach Henderson took several wide steps backward, away from Ellie. Then the coach tossed the ball toward her in a high underhand arc.

Ellie watched the ball as it fell toward her but realized too late that it was angled slightly to her right. With her weight already on her right foot, she couldn't move quickly enough to get under it in time.

The ball fell to the floor and bounced away. Ellie's heart began pounding. She suddenly felt eyes staring at her, judging her mistake.

"Oops!" Coach Henderson said as Ellie jogged over to retrieve the rolling ball.

Ellie hoped that she'd turned away in time to hide the blushing.

"I should have started with another very important part of setting," Coach Henderson said. "Perfect hand position can't help you without solid footwork. While you are waiting to set, make sure your hips are squared at the target."

The girls looked on.

Coach Henderson pointed between herself and an imaginary target. "Be ready to get underneath that ball quickly before you even put your arms up," she said. "Ellie, you toss the ball to me this time."

Ellie obeyed, and Coach Henderson bent her knees, shuffling briskly underneath the falling ball. She caught it briefly on her fingertips and then pushed it back toward Ellie in a perfect set.

Ellie was still standing right next to the net. She saw her opportunity. Instead of catching the ball, she jumped up and spiked it down onto the other side with a bang.

The team cheered.

Ellie grinned, and her embarrassment faded. She still had it.

CHAPTER 2

PLAYING IN THE PARK

When Ellie came out of the locker room after practice, Isabella was waiting for her in the hall. The neighborhood they both lived in was not far from the school, and they always walked together. The girls pushed open the school's heavy front doors and went out into the afternoon sunshine.

"I think we have a good team this year," Isabella said cheerfully.

"If I can learn not to make a fool of myself setting, maybe," Ellie said, only half joking. She still couldn't believe she'd messed up in front of the whole team during a demonstration. She shook her head and sighed.

"Everybody messes up sometimes," Isabella said, waving her hand. "You'll be fine! And half the team is new, anyway. They aren't going to judge you!"

"True," Ellie said, smiling. "I hope they settle in soon, though. Some of them were looking pretty nervous during that three-on-three battle drill!"

"Well, it was only the first day . . ." Isabella said, trailing off.

Ellie looked over to see what she was staring at. They were passing a small neighborhood park with a playground and a patchy baseball field. On one edge of the field was an old sand volleyball court.

Ellie had never seen anyone in that court except for toddlers digging, but today there was a small group of girls bunched in the middle, talking quietly.

They looked like they were maybe eight or nine years old and very serious. There was a rope tied up between the two empty posts, and one of the girls was clutching a soccer ball.

As Ellie and Isabella watched, the girls spread out three to a side and began to play what looked like an attempt at volleyball. One girl held the soccer ball out in her hand and served it over the rope. Her friends on the other side scrambled toward it, but they got in each other's way. The ball fell harmlessly into the sand.

Isabella and Ellie looked at each other, and without a word they turned and walked toward the court. The same girl served again. This time one of her friends was able to thump the ball back over the net, but it went immediately out of bounds, rolling onto the sidewalk toward Ellie's feet.

She scooped it up and tossed it back to the girls, who had all turned to look at them.

"Hi," Ellie said. "Do you mind if we watch? We love volleyball."

"We're not playing very well," said the girl who had served. "This old beach court is kind of weird." She kicked at the sand.

"We can't get into the gym anymore," another taller girl piped up. She pointed to a large building on the other side of the park. "Basketball players are using it all the time. They won't let us put up a net."

"That's terrible," Isabella said. "Did you use to have a place to play in the gym?"

"Yeah," the first girl said, sighing. "But the volunteer coach moved away a couple of weeks ago. She said she would find someone to take over our practices, but nobody ever came. When we came today, the sign on the gym just said free play instead of volleyball."

"What is that place?" Ellie asked, nodding at the large building across the park. She had never walked over to that side of the park before or even really noticed that building.

"It's a Boys & Girls Club," the second girl explained. "We go there after school to play or do homework. They have games and computers and stuff. We miss volleyball, though."

"I bet you do!" Ellie told her. "We play volleyball at the junior high, and we love it. We would be sad, too, if our coach went away." She exchanged a look with Isabella and then dropped her backpack on the grass. "Do you want us to show you some fun practice games you can play, even without a net?"

The girls perked up immediately. "Really?" the taller girl said, looking surprised. "Thanks!"

"What's your name?" Ellie asked the girl as she handed over the ball.

"Val," the girl replied, smiling shyly.

"Hi, Val," Ellie said, smiling back. "I'm Ellie, and this is Isabella."

With those introductions out of the way, Ellie went around the group, pointing to each girl in turn to get her name. Then she motioned for them to follow her onto the firmer park grass.

"Val, Eva, and Noelle, line up over here and spread out," she said, pointing. "I'm going to show you a ladder passing drill. Once you get it, the other three can take turns bumping, and then you can all switch places. Ready?"

The girls all nodded.

Isabella chimed in, "Just wait a second. You all know the difference between a bump and a set, right?"

The girls nodded again, but more slowly this time. A couple of them searched each other's faces and generally looked unsure.

Ellie smiled at her friend. "Thanks, Isabella. Let's back up a little bit. We'll *show* you what you're going to be doing, then I'll do it with you three first."

The two friends got into position so they faced each other, about ten feet apart. "I'm going to bump the ball to Isabella, and she's going to set it back to me," Ellie said.

She took a ready stance and tossed the ball straight up into the air. She put her arms straight out in front of her, hands together with thumbs flat on top. As the ball fell, she raised her fingertips upward to meet it.

The ball made a smooth arc through the air to where Isabella waited in a setter's position. Isabella's spread fingers met the ball softly overhead, pushing it back toward Ellie.

They repeated this a few times, and then Ellie caught the ball and turned to face the girls. After a quick explanation of the ladder drill, they began.

Ellie got into her ready stance and bumped the ball to Val. Val did a pretty nice job setting it back in the right direction. Ellie was able to shuffle beneath it and bump it to Eva.

Eva did set the ball, but it went a little wild, and Ellie had to scramble. She got to it in time, though, and bumped it toward Noelle.

Since she was off balance, Ellie bumped the ball a little too far. It flew past the outstretched fingers of Noelle. Ellie quickly ran off to retrieve the ball as it rolled toward the playground. *At least that wasn't my fault,* she reassured herself. *They're just kids.*

Isabella said, "Not bad for a first try, girls! Do you get the idea?"

The girls nodded and smiled.

"You can also just take turns bumping it back and forth to each other if the moving part is too hard," said Isabella. "Add that moving part later."

After a few more rounds, Ellie handed the ball back to Noelle. "Have fun, girls," she said. "Maybe we'll see you out here again sometime."

As Ellie and Isabella walked away, they heard the younger girls chattering behind them.

"That was fun," Isabella said. "You know, to help them out like that."

"Yeah," said Ellie. "Those girls definitely have the heart to play. But what are they going to do without a coach?"

CHAPTER 3

ELLIE'S BIG IDEA

Ellie pushed her potatoes around the plate. She couldn't stop thinking about those sweet kids in the park and how fun it had been to help them. She began to imagine what it would feel like if she wanted to play volleyball but couldn't. At first it made her sad, and then she began to get a little angry.

"You're awfully quiet tonight, Ellie-Belly," her mom said finally, poking her gently in the ribs to get her attention.

"Sorry, Mom," Ellie said, coming back to the present.

Her parents looked at her with curiousity.

"Trouble at practice?" Dad asked.

"No, nothing like that," Ellie said quickly. "Isabella and I met some little kids in the park today. They were trying to play volleyball on that old sand court."

"Goodness, I don't think I've ever seen anyone use that thing," Mom said.

"Yeah, it's in pretty bad shape," Ellie agreed. "They used to play in that Boys & Girls Club over there, but their coach was a volunteer, and she left. We showed them some stuff today, but I don't know how long it'll keep them busy."

Ellie's parents exchanged a glance.

Ellie sighed. "They didn't even have a real ball to play with!" she said.

"It's really nice that you want to help them, honey," Dad said. "I think our neighbor Jim used to volunteer over at that club. Maybe he could talk to you about how it works."

Ellie perked up. "Am I even old enough to do that?" she asked. "Don't you have to be an adult or something?"

"Maybe Coach Henderson would be willing to help you figure something out," Mom suggested. "It can't hurt to ask, right?"

"Right!" Ellie agreed, starting to feel much better. Coach would definitely know what to do.

* * *

On Thursday, Ellie showed up even earlier for practice. Coach Henderson hadn't even gotten the net out of the storage closet yet.

As she helped the coach get the gym ready for practice, Ellie explained her encounter with the kids. She told how she really wanted to find a way to help them. Coach Henderson listened as she talked.

"My parents said maybe we could volunteer. But we need a grownup to help," she explained.

"You know, Ellie," Coach Henderson said finally, "I was just reading an article about how junior coaching can be a great tool for learning," She paused, looking thoughtful. "It's a big commitment, though."

"I know it is. But if a lot of us took turns, it wouldn't be so much, right?" Ellie said. She tried hard not to sound like she was begging. But the more she talked about it, the more she wanted this plan to work out.

"Well, it is very good practice for you girls to approach skills from a different viewpoint. And giving back to the sport and helping future players is a wonderful thing to do."

Ellie looked at her hopefully. "Does that mean you'll help?" she asked.

"Actually, I think volunteer coaching might be just what the team needs. We can set up some kind of kids volleyball practice hour or something over there and have you girls take turns helping me. Let's ask everyone else what they think."

Ellie's heart soared. As soon as Isabella came through the gym door, she ran over to share the good news. "She'll help us! Coach Henderson is going to help us set up volunteer volleyball coaching at the club!" she reported, hopping with excitement.

Her happiness was contagious. By the time Coach Henderson explained how a volunteer junior coaching program might work, half the team was ready to join in on the plan.

"Now, it will depend on a few things. We need to find out the available gym schedule at the club and how many of you can commit," Coach Henderson cautioned. "And of course we'll need your parent's permission. But if you are all on board with the idea, I'll be happy to help."

The gym filled with chatter.

Many of the girls couldn't wait to get started, but some of them were unsure about the idea of coaching. The new girls were especially worried about teaching a game they were just learning themselves. Others said they would need to know the schedule before they could agree.

Coach promised she'd get them more information as soon as she had talked to the volunteer organizers at the Boys & Girls Club. But now it was time for the team's own practice to begin.

CHAPTER 4

SIDELINED

The serve arced straight toward Ellie, who held her arms out to meet it with a solid, confident thump. Her dig popped the ball into the air, and Isabella centered herself below it near the net, ready to set. Her raised fingers met the ball and pushed it toward their teammate Anna, who attacked with a powerful hit. The ball flew over the net and straight toward a hole in the back row on the opposite side.

Point for the Cheetahs.

It was the first match of the year, and so far they were on fire. The match was the best out of three, and they had already won the first game, 25-14. Now, in the second game, they were already way up again, scoring ten points to their opponents' three. The Bluebells had been a good team last year, but now they just seemed like they were still warming up.

Ellie was feeling strong and bold in the back row, digging out everything the other team hit at them without even breaking a sweat. She grinned as she watched the ball soar through the air. This was fun.

The Cheetahs' next serve flew over the net, but a tall Bluebell with a long ponytail dug the ball up just in time. The setter received the pass and took a big step to the right, pivoting to face her target. She raised her hands and set the ball directly to her hitter with a flick of her wrists. The Bluebells' hitter was ready and made the attack.

Isabella was right there at the net, ready and waiting to block. She leapt high, and the ball deflected off her outstretched hands and back to the Bluebells' side, landing inbounds.

Ellie and her teammates cheered the point.

After another point, Anna missed a set, giving the Bluebells a side out. The serve switched, but the Cheetahs got their own side out again when a Bluebell serve went into the net.

The rotation took Ellie into the front row, and Isabella moved into the back to serve. Isabella sent the ball low over the net. An outside hitter on the Bluebells dug it up and sent the ball straight back over the net.

Ellie hadn't been prepared to block so soon. She managed to get an arm in front of the ball, but she hadn't reacted quickly enough. The ball went straight into the net, and the other team whooped, high-fiving all around. Anna and Ally patted Ellie on the back before jogging into position again.

The Bluebells rotated, their new server bouncing the ball loudly on the floor a few times before sending it over the net. It headed straight to Isabella, who dug it out with an awkward bump that sent the ball high up into the rafters of the gymnasium.

Luckily, Ally had time to chase it down and set it to Ellie. Ellie tipped it over the net, but the Bluebells rallied easily, sending it back over with a nasty spike right at Ellie's feet.

Point for the Bluebells.

Ellie's stomach twisted. She had been feeling good about this game early on. Suddenly things didn't seem to be going her way at all. She heard the whistle for a time out, and Coach Henderson motioned for a substitution.

"Come take a break, Ellie," Coach Henderson said kindly. "Let Dawn try her hand in the front row for a while."

Ellie tried not to take it personally. But anyone could see she was rattled and making a lot of mistakes. She watched the next few rallies from the bench, working hard to fight back her worry and cheer on the team.

Isabella rotated to the front row again, and Ally set her up for a beautiful hit. The ball cleared the net, zipped past the blockers, and went straight to the floor.

Ellie clapped and shouted loudly for her friends. Had she been benched long enough? *Am I ever going to get subbed back in?* she wondered. *I hope Coach Henderson isn't mad at me.*

As she watched, trying not to worry, the next serve went over the net low and fast. The Bluebells returned it easily. In the backcourt, Dawn dug it up and sent the ball toward Isabella in the front row. Instead of setting, though, Isabella dumped it straight over the net in a surprise attack.

The Bluebells' blocker was right there. She hit it back immediately, almost in Isabella's face.

Anna, inexperienced and overreacting to the unexpected volley, had crowded up right behind

Isabella, who didn't see her. They both leapt to block the returning ball at the same time and collided, falling together into the net and then to the floor. The ball bounced away as both girls cried out in pain.

The game stopped with a loud shriek of the referee's whistle.

Ellie rushed forward with her teammates to link arms in a privacy wall around their fallen friends. Coach joined the circle to check their injuries. Ellie's heart pounded in her chest as she waited to find out what was wrong. Seconds began to feel like hours.

Anna was the first one to emerge from the circle, crying and clutching a bloody tissue to her nose. She had taken an elbow to the face, but she was going to be okay.

Finally Isabella got to her feet and came out of the circle, leaning heavily on Coach Henderson's shoulder and hopping on her right foot.

"It's my ankle," Isabella sniffled. "I think it's broken." She held her left foot gingerly in the air as she made her way over to the bench.

"Probably just a sprain," reassured Coach Henderson. "But we'll get some ice on it right now. Ellie, would you please call her mother?"

Ellie ran off to get her phone from the locker room, feeling terrible for her friend — and for her team.

Even if Isabella's ankle isn't broken, how long will it be until she can play again after such a bad injury? Ellie wondered. A front row rock star like Isabella needed her jump! This season was looking worse all of a sudden.

CHAPTER 5

THE BOYS & GIRLS CLUB

At the next practice on Tuesday, Isabella sat on the bleachers with a bandaged ankle. She looked grumpy about it, but she wasn't going to miss practice just because of a sprain.

"Well girls, the bad news is that Isabella's going to be sticking to the sidelines for a few weeks while she recovers," Coach Henderson announced. "But I do have some good news too. I spoke with the volunteer coordinator at the Boys & Girls Club, and we can start a youth volleyball club on Wednesdays after school."

Ellie's heart jumped. That meant the first practice would start tomorrow!

"I'm not going to make it required, but I do encourage everyone who is able to join us," Coach Henderson said. "Coaching is fun, but it's also a wonderful way to build your own skills by looking at them from a new perspective." She handed around a stack of permission forms.

Isabella raised her hand. "Can I still come help, even though I can't play right now?" she asked.

"Of course!" said Coach Henderson. "A sprained ankle won't keep you from helping. There is still plenty you can do. Look at me — I do a lot more talking than playing, and you still keep me around, right?" She winked at Isabella, who smiled and sat up straighter.

"I think we'll try taking turns at the club in pairs of two, at least to start," Coach Henderson suggested. "That way everyone gets a chance to pitch in and gain some experience."

"Can we go more often if we want to?" Ellie asked. The club was right by her house, after all. She had been looking forward to getting to know the girls — and she was sure the extra practice wasn't going to hurt either.

"Sure," Coach Henderson agreed, "you can tag along as often as you'd like to. But two at a time will be the official rotation."

Ally nominated Ellie and Isabella as the lead junior coaches for the first practice, since the club had been their idea. Everyone agreed that this was a good plan.

* * *

The next school day felt extra long. In math class, her last period of the day, Ellie stared at the clock for what felt like hours, urging it to move faster. When the bell finally rang, she popped out of her seat and raced to meet Isabella at her locker.

Because Isabella couldn't walk very well on her sprained ankle, the two friends rode with Coach Henderson over to the club. There was a big sign on the front door announcing the new volleyball club. Ellie was thrilled when she saw it — but also a bit more nervous. This was real!

"I hope the equipment is okay," Coach Henderson said as they approached the big blue doors of the gym. "I only had a chance to take a quick look at it when I came by on Saturday."

The gymnasium was smaller than the one at their school and had no bleachers, but it was clean and well lit. A couple of young boys were playing basketball on one end of the court. They stopped and watched as Ellie, Isabella, and Coach Henderson walked to the supply closet and opened the door wide. Together they dragged the net and a bag of balls out onto the floor.

"Are you going to stay for the volleyball club?" Ellie asked them with a friendly smile.

"Um, no," the taller boy said.

"Well, you're welcome if you want to join us," Coach Henderson added as she locked the first pole into the floor port. "It's open to any kid at the club. We start today."

"Maybe we'll come back later," the boy said, looking a little annoyed. "I don't know how to play volleyball." He and his friend bounced their basketball around a few more times before they finally left.

"I hope we get some takers!" Isabella said. "What if nobody shows up?"

"Val and her friends will be here at least," Ellie said. "I just know it. They were so sad about not being able to play anymore."

Sure enough, when the net was hung, and Isabella had just finished inflating the last ball, the door popped open with a squeak. The same young girls that had been playing in the park walked in. They looked nervous and excited.

There were a couple of new girls along with them too.

"Hi! Welcome!" Ellie said, running over to greet them.

"I can't believe it," Val exclaimed. "You got us a new coach!"

"And we get to help coach too," Ellie said as Isabella waved from the bleachers.

After introductions and a quick warm-up drill, Coach Henderson turned to Ellie and Isabella. "Why don't you girls start with a setting demonstration?" she suggested.

Ellie's stomach did an unexpected flip. She had been having issues with setting, and Isabella had to stay seated. *What if I make a fool of myself in front of the girls?* she worried.

"There are many different skills involved in volleyball," Coach Henderson said. "We'll start with hand position and technique for setting. The great thing about this drill is that it's something you can even practice at home all by yourself. Isabella will demonstrate throwing the ball up and catching it with proper form."

Isabella limped to the middle of the floor and settled herself cross-legged in front of the net. She held the ball loosely and tossed it gently a few feet into the air. Spreading her fingers and elbows wide, she caught it just above her forehead, using only her fingertips. She popped it back into the air and caught it perfectly a second time, then a third.

"See how her shoulders are open, fingers spread, and she's not touching the ball with her palms at all?" Coach Henderson explained. "That's just what I want you all to do. But before we start, let me show you what we'll be doing after that. Ellie?" Coach beckoned Ellie.

Ellie joined Isabella by the net.

Coach Henderson continued. "Can you partner with Isabella, so she's setting to you? At ten feet for ten sets, then fifteen feet, and so on?"

Ellie nodded, relieved. Catching Isabella's sets wasn't anything to be nervous about. She and Isabella got in position

Coach Henderson said, "You take over and explain what you're doing now."

Ellie took a deep breath. "Okay, girls," she said, turning to the group, "Isabella is going to keep the same form, but she's going to aim out a little bit so that the ball flies up and over to me."

Ellie pushed her arms straight up at an imaginary ball, then out at an angle to show them the difference. "Her target will be somewhere about here." She drew an X high in the air between them with her finger.

Isabella tossed the ball up and set it. Ellie caught it easily. "See how she straightened her elbows in a nice, clean follow-through? That helps push the ball in the direction you want it to go."

The younger girls nodded their heads. They kept their eyes on Ellie, waiting for what was next.

"Let's pair off and try that ten times," Ellie said, smiling. She was really enjoying this coaching thing. "When you have the hang of it, take a couple of big steps back, so you're about this far away."

Ellie moved back, and Isabella set the ball to her again. "Now the angle of her arms is a little bit lower, because she needs to push the ball out more than up. Can you see that?" Ellie asked. The girls nodded again. "Okay, let's try it!"

Isabella climbed to her feet and hobbled over to the balls. She handed them out, and Ellie helped the girls get settled in their spots. There was a lot of giggling at first as balls bounced off foreheads instead of fingers. Some of the balls flew too far and rolled off toward their neighbors.

Ellie and Coach Henderson walked around gently correcting positions and giving advice. Ellie noticed Val catching the ball neatly, but it was settling deep in her hands, not in her fingertips.

"If you catch it like that, you won't be able to set it cleanly," Ellie explained to her. "In a game, you might be charged with carrying." She moved Val's hands into a narrower position and placed the ball in between them. "Can you feel the difference?"

Val nodded, and Ellie smiled. "Now try it again," she said.

Val tossed the ball up in the air and caught it in her fingertips, just as Ellie had shown her.

"Awesome!" Ellie said. "I think you've got the idea!"

Suggesting this club was the best idea I've had in a long time, she thought proudly. Helping the kids learn the sport she loved was as much fun as it was good practice. Her own problems on the volleyball court seemed long ago and far away.

CHAPTER 6

SETTING STRUGGLES

Ellie arrived at volleyball practice the next afternoon full of energy. She was excited to tell her teammates how well the first club meeting had gone.

"It was funny to see them making the same mistakes I made when I was first learning how to play," she explained to Ally. "And it was cool that I knew what to say to help them fix errors."

Practice began with a game of volleyball tag to warm up. Isabella played referee since she was still off her feet. Coach Henderson was *it* first.

Staying within the lines on half the court, the girls raced and dodged to avoid being tagged.

As they ran around, they tossed volleyballs between them. Whoever held the ball was safe, so they worked together to pass it quickly to teammates in immediate danger. The ball flew back and forth like lightning. They enjoyed a good three minutes of avoiding the coach's tags before she finally got Ally while the ball was in the air.

By the time the game was over, everyone was out of breath. They ran through some stretching and some simple skill drills next.

"Okay, everyone gather over by the net," Coach finally called. "Abby, Ellie, help me hang up these blankets." She held up two sheets and bunch of clips.

"So we're covering the net with *blankets*?" Ellie asked, confused.

"Yep," Coach Henderson said. "We're playing a new game today. Blind Volleyball."

Several girls started asking questions.

"But how can we play without being able to see the other team?" Anna said loudest, a little panic in her voice.

"Playing blind will help you focus on working more closely with the team on your own side of net," Coach Henderson explained. "With the other team out of sight, you can practice reading your own half of the court. Don't worry. It'll be fun."

When the blankets were hung, they divided into two groups. Coach subbed in for Isabella on Ellie's team. The first serve came over the net, and Ellie dug it out of the back row. Ally, already showing talent for setting, made a nice clean contact, hips and feet pointed at the best-positioned hitter. Dawn was there to spike the ball over the net cleanly.

It felt strange to wait for the ball to come back without being able to see where it would come from, so Ellie just tried to stay alert and ready.

Sure enough, just after the third thump, it sailed straight from the right side of the net to the back row. Again, Ellie was there for the pass.

Soon, though, Coach Henderson switched Ellie to setting. Unfortunately for Ellie, the issues she had been having before popped up right away. First, it was a bad set that flew so far to the right of her intended target that it left the court. Next, she paid so much attention to the ball that she knocked into a teammate. After that, she set one way too high for the hitter.

Coach Henderson stopped the action. "Ellie," she said, "your form looks great when you're in the back row digging. But when you're setting, you need to make sure you're watching your hitters. You want those sets to stay right here in this zone, about three to five feet off the net. Got it?"

Ellie nodded in agreement, but she felt her face reddening.

"When the ball comes to you, you need to know where you're putting it," Coach Henderson continued. "Focus on staying high and using those last two steps to square up to your inside target. Does that make sense?"

Ellie nodded, frowning. She didn't like being the focus of so much correction.

The ball didn't come to her at all on the next rally, and on the third, she was trying so hard to focus on the hitters that she was late getting underneath the ball. She made contact, but it was sloppy. The ball bounced off to one side, away from the hitter.

Ellie stomped her foot, huffing loudly.

Coach Henderson walked over to Ellie. "Take a deep breath, Ellie," said Coach Henderson softly. "It's just practice."

Ellie tried to calm down, but she was getting frustrated. When she was in the back row, the game seemed easy to her. She could see the ball coming and knew exactly what to do to help her team. In the front row, she just couldn't seem to juggle all the different things she needed to pay attention to.

"Can I just go back to passing?" Ellie asked with a sigh.

Coach Henderson raised her eyebrows. "Everyone on the team should understand and be comfortable with the basics, even if you have a favorite position," she said. "Not only that, but Isabella is out for a few weeks at least. We need players who are able to step in when a teammate is down."

Ellie nodded though it wasn't what she wanted to hear. Coach Henderson jogged back to middle-hitter position and called out for the other team to serve.

The rest of practice was a mixed bag. Ellie managed to place a few more of her sets where the attackers could get a good hit on them.

A lot of her sets had too much spin, however, and she was often late to the ball.

She left the gym feeling grumpy and defeated. *Who am I to teach volleyball,* she thought, *when I can't even get my own act together?*

CHAPTER 7

COACHING CLUES

"Please come with me," Ally begged the following week. "Abby's home sick today, and I don't know these girls yet, and I'm nervous."

Ellie sighed. She really wasn't feeling up to going to the club this week, not when she was so frustrated with her own volleyball struggles. But her friend's begging was wearing her down. And she hated the thought of letting down those happy little girls.

"Did you ask Isabella?" said Ellie. "She was there last week too."

"Yes, but she has a doctor's appointment for her ankle," Ally said, sighing. "Will you please, please, *please* come?"

"Okay, I'll be there," Ellie said finally. "But there's nothing to be afraid of. You're awesome at volleyball, and the kids are really sweet."

"I know, I know," Ally said. "It will just be so much better if you're there."

* * *

When they arrived at the Boys & Girls Club that afternoon, Coach Henderson was pulling the net and balls out of the closet. Val was there too and waved at Ellie as soon as she walked in the door.

"Look, Ellie. We brought some friends!" Val chirped, bouncing over to say hello.

"I brought a friend too," Ellie told her, smiling. "This is Ally. She's going to be helping coach you guys this week."

With everyone's help, they quickly cleared out the gym and set up the net.

"For warm-up, can we teach them volleyball tag?" Ally asked Coach Henderson. "That's super fun to play."

"Great idea," Coach Henderson agreed. "Why don't you take the lead on that?"

"It's just like regular tag, except the crowd has a volleyball," Ally explained to the girls. "I'll be it first. The it can't tag you if you have the ball. But don't just keep it. Throw the ball quickly to whoever is about to be tagged, okay? You're a team working against me."

The game began. Even running slowly, Ally made her first tag pretty fast, but the girls didn't seem to mind. They were shrieking with laughter as they tried to beat their friends' tags with the ball.

Watching from the sidelines as a referee, Ellie saw that the girls were often too preoccupied running from whoever was it to notice the throw in time to catch it. Often, whoever scooped it up next took too long to figure out which player was in danger and needed it most. All of the running and shrieking definitely added to the confusion. But at least they were having fun.

After a few minutes of this, Coach Henderson blew the whistle and called everyone over for the first drill of the day. "Today we're going to pair up and practice setting," she said. "Ellie, can you please demonstrate setting position? Show them the hips method."

Ellie felt her stomach churn at the mention of setting. She hid it with a nod and put her hands on her waist with her fingers spread wide. Keeping them the same distance apart, she raised her thumbs to her forehead, elbows to the side. This left her fingers spaced just far enough for a ball to fit between them.

The little girls all did the same thing.

Coach Henderson walked down the line adjusting their hands a bit. She turned to Ellie and said, "Now, can you and Ally please show the girls how to set back and forth over the net? Start close, and then slowly move farther apart."

Ally jogged over to the other side of the court. Ellie tossed the ball straight up in the air and then set it. The ball sailed smoothly over to Ally, who expertly sent it back.

They managed a few clean volleys, but then Ally got a little off balance while stepping back and sent the ball wild.

Ellie scooted beneath it. She bumped it up in the air to herself to get it back in position to play and then set it back to Ally.

"Nice, Ellie!" Coach Henderson said. "I know most of you girls are new to this, but if you can do something like that to keep the ball in play, go ahead and try it! Just keep it going back and forth as long as you can."

Ellie caught the ball on the next volley and helped divide the girls up into pairs. Not all of them could fit at the net, so she took a few over to the baselines to use it as a marker instead.

Coach Henderson and the JV players wandered the room, helping the girls with the drill. First, Ellie showed Val how if she held her hands a little closer together, the ball would bounce neatly off her fingertips instead of sinking down to her palms.

"You want all your fingers to touch the ball, but nothing else, see?" Ellie explained, demonstrating a few sets.

Val nodded, and Ellie moved on.

"Okay, Maya," Ellie said, walking over to another little girl. The girl had been pushing at the ball in a way that made it fly straight at her partner rather than arcing through the air. "You want to position your hands so that the volleyball would hit you right between the eyes if you let it go through your fingers. See? Up here." Ellie gently moved the girl's hands up higher.

Maya tried again, and this time the ball sailed up in a gentle curve.

"Awesome!" Ellie said.

Across the gym, another pair, Nicole and Emily, practiced. Their ball flew all over the place. They managed just a volley or two before the ball would fly off, forcing them to chase it.

Ellie walked closer to watch what they were doing. As she approached, she saw Coach Henderson also heading in the same direction. The coach smiled and waved Ellie forward, turning instead to talk to another girl who had just dropped the ball.

"Hi, girls! Having fun?" Ellie said as Emily missed the ball yet again, running off to chase it.

"Sort of," Nicole said, giggling. "But we can't do more than three or four hits before the ball goes all over the room!"

"Want some help with that?" Ellie offered.

"Yes, please!" Nicole said.

Emily returned with the ball, out of breath.

"Okay. I see a few things I can help with," said Ellie. "One reason your sets are flying all over the place is because there is so much spin on the ball. You're doing a good job using only your fingertips, but I think maybe you need to use all of your fingers. That way you have more control over where the ball goes. Does that make sense?"

The two girls nodded.

Ellie tossed the ball a few times to demonstrate the difference in the way the ball moved with and without spin. "The other thing I see is that when you're chasing the ball, you're facing the ball itself and not the place you want to set it. If you square up and face your partner when you set, the ball will go straight back to her. Want to try again?"

Emily and Nicole nodded and spread out. This time they managed four sets before the ball went wide. Emily ran underneath it, turning sideways to scurry as it fell so that she was still facing Nicole. This time her set went straight to its target.

"Amazing, Emily!" Ellie said, clapping. She glanced over at Coach Henderson, who was standing off to the side, watching Ellie work. The coach flashed her a big smile and a thumbs up.

After a few more volleys, Nicole dropped the ball, but she was grinning broadly. "That was better!" she exclaimed.

"You'll get the hang of this," Ellie said.

As she walked away, she kept thinking about what she'd seen. Facing where you wanted the ball to go sounded so easy when she explained it. Maybe her setting problems weren't so complicated after all. *If only I could figure out how to take my own advice!*

CHAPTER 8

ISABELLA'S ANSWER

Ellie lay on the floor of Isabella's basement. She set a volleyball straight up into the air to herself, over and over. Isabella was on the couch above her, flexing her ankle. She no longer wore the Ace bandage and had been given some physical therapy exercises to begin getting back in shape for volleyball. She was still not allowed to run or jump yet.

"The doctor said maybe only a couple more weeks before I can play again," Isabella said. "As long as I take care of it in the meantime."

"That's great," Ellie said, sounding distracted. She continued tossing the ball to herself.

"Why are you so quiet?" Isabella finally asked her, after a long silence.

"I'm sorry," Ellie said. "Ugh. Volleyball is so frustrating lately. I can't seem to do anything right at practice. But when I watch the kids at the Boys & Girls Club, I can totally see what they are doing wrong. And I think some of it is the same stuff."

"Like what?" Isabella asked, pointing her toes to the ceiling.

"I know I have the hand position right," said Ellie. "But I think my footwork is the biggest problem. Especially when I'm setting."

Isabella was quiet for a minute, thinking. Then she said, "You know, when I was first learning volleyball, I practiced footwork like a dance. I found some songs that had the right beat for the different steps and practiced down here a lot."

"You did?" Ellie said, surprised. "Why didn't you ever tell me about this? I would've practiced with you!"

"That was before you joined the team," Isabella reminded her. "We weren't best friends yet. But I definitely think it helped. Want to try it?"

"Of course I do!" said Ellie.

Isabella got up and walked carefully over to a stereo in the corner. "I wish I could show you, but I'll just have to talk you through it. The best music for this was these weird old cha-cha CDs my dad has down here."

"Whatever works," said Ellie.

Isabella popped something into the music player. "Stand over here and pretend that wall is the net," she said, pointing to the largest open area in the room.

Ellie scrambled to her feet and stood in a ready position, as if she were facing the left antenna of the volleyball net, about to set.

Isabella continued, "You know how the setting footwork goes right-left and then a little ready hop, where you square up?" She pretended to set a volleyball in the air above her forehead. "Those will be beats one, two, and three. Beat four is the pause. Then you do the steps back to your starting position. Does that make sense?"

"I think so," Ellie said. She pretended she was getting ready to set and took two big steps to the side, then a quick double step to square herself to the invisible antenna again. "Can I hear the music now, Isabella?"

Isabella started the music, and the first few bars of a mellow cha-cha filled the room. Ellie listened for a few beats and then began to move with the music.

"Right, left, ready! Left, right, ready!" she murmured as she leapt back and forth across the room, setting imaginary balls to imaginary hitters. Isabella clapped along to the beat.

When the song ended, Isabella stopped the music with the touch of a button. "That looked good!" Isabella said. "How did it feel?"

"Fun!" Ellie said, laughing. "We should have music at all our practices."

"Want another song?" Isabella asked.

"Yes, but can you point out targets for me, to mix it up?" Ellie asked. "I need to practice not knowing where the ball will be too."

"Totally," Isabella agreed. "Oh, wait! I have an even better idea. We can do the cone thing."

One of the practic drills the team did involved the coach tossing a tennis ball into the air while the players held small traffic cones to their foreheads, similar to a setting hand position. The girls had to try to catch the ball inside the cone.

"I love that game," said Ellie.

Isabella rummaged around in a bin, coming back with an old party hat and a ping pong ball. "This will work!" she said, laughing.

Isabella started the music again and sat on the couch. As she tossed the ball, Ellie scooted beneath it, trying to keep her footwork squared up. The ball plopped into the hat with a satisfying *tock*.

Three songs into this new practice game, Isabella's mom called down the stairs.

"Ellie! Your mom just asked me to send you home," she said kindly. "Isabella, our dinner is almost ready too. Come clean up."

Isabella stopped the music, and Ellie picked up her backpack.

"Thanks!" Ellie said, a little out of breath. "That was awesome. I'm going to do that every day when I get home until I nail this setting thing.

* * *

The next week at practice was an encouraging one. Ellie still felt a lot stronger playing in the back row as a passer than in the front as a setter, but all the footwork practice was definitely starting to make a difference. She still made mistakes, but her heart didn't jump into her throat every time she rotated to a new position anymore.

"Wow, great job getting to the ball so quickly, Ellie!" Coach Henderson said when Ellie managed a decent set. "You're really starting to get that footwork down."

Ellie glanced over at Isabella, who was doing low-impact exercises on the sidelines. They grinned at each other but didn't explain the secret method.

Maybe I'll suggest it to Coach for the kids to try later, Ellie thought.

CHAPTER 9

CHEETAHS VS. COMETS

Ellie pulled the knot tight on her shoelace and headed out of the locker room to the gym. The match was beginning soon. Parents already speckled the bleachers.

"Ellie!" someone shouted.

Ellie glanced over and saw Val waving madly. Three other girls from the Boys & Girls Club were also sitting in the front row. Isabella was sitting with them in her uniform.

"Hi, guys!" Ellie said, jogging over. "I didn't know you were coming to the game!"

"Last week, Coach Henderson told us we should come and watch if we could," Val explained. "My sister brought us." She pointed to a teenager looking at her phone behind them. She looked up and gave Ellie a polite wave.

"Well, thanks for coming," Ellie told them. "I hope you enjoy the game!"

"I had a doctor's appointment this afternoon," Isabella said, grinning. "They said I should be able to start playing again next week!"

Ellie squealed and threw her arms around her friend.

Minutes later, the game began. A coin toss determined that the Comets would serve first. In the back row, Ellie bounced lightly in her ready position, watching the server. When the ball arced over the net, she scooted a step to the left and passed it neatly to Ally with a solid bump.

Ally set the ball to Anna in the left front. Anna hit it back over the net, where the other team managed a pass and set. The hitter was late to the ball, though, and the return shot bounced harmlessly off the net.

Side-out and a point for the Cheetahs!

Ellie was the first to serve for her team. Her ball sailed over the net cleanly. The Comets tried to dump it back over the net, but Dawn was there with a block. The ball bounced to the floor between the left front and middle hitters.

Another point!

Ellie could hear the younger girls in the stands cheering wildly. She gave them a quick little wave.

After a couple more successful rallies, the Comets managed to dump a short shot right in front of Abby for a side out.

A tall girl with a strong overhand serve drilled the ball over the net — just barely. It brushed the top of the net, but it wasn't enough to stop it or slow it down very much.

Ellie was ready to go.

She threw herself quickly to the side and stopped it with a forearm bump. She didn't have a lot of control over the pass, but it worked. Ally was able to get under it and set to Dawn, who spiked it back over the net.

It was a quick game. The Comets managed some decent shots, but they just couldn't seem to return enough volleys. The serve stayed mostly on the Cheetahs' side of the court. The first game ended with a score of 25-11.

The team gathered on the sidelines for a quick water break between games. Coach Henderson was giving hugs all around.

"You have so much hustle tonight," the coach said, putting an arm around Ellie. "It's amazing. Do you think we can put some of that energy into setting this time? You've improved so very much lately."

Ellie nodded, smiling to hide her nervousness. She'd been practicing her footwork every day and was feeling a lot more confident. If Coach Henderson thought she was ready for some front row action, well, maybe she was.

Game two started off well enough. Ally, Abby, Rachel, and Dawn were sitting on the bench this time. Emma, Kaitlyn, Grace, and Olivia were on the court instead. The other team also seemed to have adjusted their positions and players.

Because they'd lost the first game, the Comets had the first serve. Ellie took a deep breath and tried to shift her focus from back row to front row mode. She watched as the serve flew over the net to Kaitlyn in the middle back.

Kaitlyn bumped it up and over toward the left side of the net, near where Ellie was positioned. Ellie took two steps back and planted herself with a quick ready hop.

Cha-cha! she sang in her head.

Ellie's fingers met the ball, and it popped into the air in front of Taylor, who hit it cleanly.

A tall player on the Comets leaped up and blocked the ball. It deflected back across the net and fell to the floor on the the Cheetahs' side of the court before anyone could react.

"No!" Ellie cried before she could stop herself. She didn't mean to be a poor sport, but the Comets were shouting in celebration anyway.

"Shake it off!" she heard Coach Henderson call to her from the sidelines.

Ellie closed her eyes for a moment and took a deep breath. *It's just a point. You didn't even mess up.*

The next serve also went to Kaitlyn, who passed it a little to Ellie's right this time. Ellie was ready and got underneath it. She set it to Taylor, who again hit it over the net.

This time, the Comets' middle hitter saved it with a dig to their setter. She set it back to the hitter for a soft shot over the net. It fell between Taylor and Olivia as they scrambled to the net.

Point for the Comets.

Ellie sighed. Once again, she waited for the serve. She tried to focus less on the other team and more on her own. The ball looped high this time, coming down near Grace, one of the new Cheetahs.

Grace bumped the ball up, but it didn't travel as far toward Ellie as the first two passes had. Ellie had to scramble to get there. When she made contact with the ball, her hands were a little too far apart. Instead of bouncing away, she felt the ball slide all the way into her palms. She knew the call before she even heard the whistle. A carry!

Ellie tried hard to stay focused and not get rattled, but it was impossible. Even playing as hard as they could, the Cheetahs never managed to score more than a couple of points in a row before the Comets would get the serve back. At the end of the second game, the Comets had prevailed by a score of 25-14.

CHAPTER 10

THE FINAL GAME

During the break, Coach Henderson changed up the lineup again. Ally was back in as setter this time. She was playing with Grace, Olivia, Abby, Rachel, and Dawn.

Once the game had started, Coach Henderson came and sat next to Ellie on the bench. "You know, Ellie, I think you should be really proud of what you did out there," she said.

Ellie looked at her and frowned. "Why?" she asked. "We lost — big time."

"Well, for one thing, we haven't lost the match yet. It's best two out of three, remember?" said Coach Henderson.

Ellie shrugged. That wasn't what she had meant, and Coach Henderson knew it.

Coach Henderson said, "Ellie, that was by far the best job I have ever seen you do as a setter, hands down. You didn't lose that game by yourself, you know. A lot of what happened out there had to do with the other team or your teammates' mistakes."

"I made plenty of mistakes out there," Ellie said softly.

"You sure did," Coach Henderson replied. "That's because you're a human. And you're still learning. But boy, are you learning! Two weeks ago, I wouldn't have considered putting you in for a whole game as a setter."

Ellie sniffled and sat up a little bit straighter.

"You really stepped it up when your team needed you," said Coach Henderson. "I hope you learn to be proud of yourself. In the meantime, I sure am proud of you."

Ellie put her head on the coach's shoulder.

Coach Henderson put her arm around Ellie for a brief moment. "Don't get too comfortable on this bench," she said as she stood up to walk away. "Ally is still new to this too, and she may get tired. Until Isabella's back, you two are the best setters I've got."

Ellie felt a bit of a smile creeping in. *I'm not perfect, but being one of the best on the team is still great,* she thought. She thought about teaching the girls at the club and all her work practicing at home. *I can do this,* she reminded herself firmly. *Face the target. Be ready with your footwork. Breathe.*

The third game seemed to be a bit more even than the first two had been. Neither team gained more than a couple of points before the other team managed to score.

With so much rotation going on, Ally was soon in the back row. Her defensive skills weren't quite as strong as her setting skills.

When it was Ally's turn to serve, the ball flew too low, hit the net, and bounced back.

Ellie winced. She hoped it didn't make Ally feel too rattled.

The other team scored the next two points by blocking Dawn's hits. Then the next serve came low and fast. Ally tried to get in front of it, but she was too slow. The ball sailed right past her and bounced away.

Olivia managed to dig up the next serve, but a hard spike after the rally kept the serve in the visitor's court. The Cheetahs were down, 17-19.

The next serve was another rocket, which slipped by Ally. The score was creeping farther out of reach, and Ally was really beginning to look upset.

Ellie heard a whistle. She looked over and saw Coach Henderson motioning to her.

I'm back in the game! Ellie thought. She took a deep breath and jogged out onto the floor.

Ellie gave Ally a quick hug as they traded places. She couldn't waste any time worrying about her friend right now, though. She needed to focus. The other team was only a few points away from taking the whole game, and they had the momentum to do it.

The serve came in low and fast. It was headed for the outside corner.

Ellie knew she couldn't get in front of it, so she dove. She got a fist under the ball and popped it up to the left front. Grace was there and set it to Dawn, who spiked it harder this time and more to the side. The ball snuck between the front row blockers and slammed against the floor.

Finally!

The girls from the club were jumping around and shouting Ellie's name. Ellie's fresh energy and determination seemed to spread to the rest of the team. Abby scored off an ace serve right away. A long rally followed on the next point, finally ending when the Comets hit it into the net. One of their players subbed out after that.

Before she knew it, Ellie was back in the front row. They were only two points from winning the game now, and the air felt electric.

Carefully, Ellie watched as the serve arced over the net to Grace, who was there to pass it to Ellie. Ellie took a big double step to the edge of the court. The ball bounced neatly off her outstretched fingertips. Rachel, seeing an opening, dumped it softly over the heads of the hitters at the net.

Only one point to go!

The next serve was a soft one. Dawn passed it. As Ellie watched the ball coming to her, she knew what she had to do.

The Comets' hitters were all clumped over in the middle and right part of the court. Ellie watched the ball falling to the left front part of the net and hopped over to meet it. But instead of setting, she hit it straight over the net.

The Comets could only watch it land inbounds with no one around.

An explosion of cheering erupted.

"Great read, Ellie!" said Coach Henderson, patting Ellie on the back.

All the girls from the club ran over from the stands and gathered around Ellie in a big, slightly overwhelming group hug. They were behaving as if Ellie was a cross between a big sister and a celebrity.

It was a sweet feeling.

ABOUT the AUTHOR

Leigh McDonald loves books! Whether she is writing them, reading them, editing them, or designing them, books are what she does best. Leigh has written several books in the Jake Maddox series, including *Dance Team Dilemma* and *Volleyball Victory*. She lives in a colorful bungalow in Tucson, Arizona, with her art teacher husband and two young daughters.

GLOSSARY

approach—the offensive player's footwork to the net before jumping to spike the ball

attack—the offensive action of hitting the ball

back row—the area on the volleyball court from the back line to the attack line

bump—to pass the volleyball using the forearms

carrying—a botched pass involving prolonged contact with the volleyball

dig—passing, usually by bumping, a fast-moving ball that is close to touching the court

front row—the area on the volleyball court from the net to the 10-foot attack line

rally—the time or number of hits between the serve and the end of the play

set—pass with the fingertips usually performed to set up a spike

scramble—to hurriedly clamber in order to reach something

shuffle—to move one's feet along without lifting them fully from the ground

stance—the way in which someone stands to get ready

DISCUSSION QUESTIONS

1. In your own words, describe Ellie's experience coaching younger girls. Talk about the ways that her experience helped her improve her own volleyball skills.

2. Doing the things we love isn't always easy. Have you ever struggled with a favorite sport or hobby? Discuss what the problem was, and what you did to get past the difficulty.

3. Helping others is important when you are part of a team. How did Ellie's teammates or coach help her out when she was having trouble? How did Ellie help her friends? Use examples from the story in your answer.

WRITING PROMPTS

1. Val and the other younger girls lost their chance to learn volleyball until Ellie and Coach Henderson helped them form a new club. Write a few paragraphs from the point of view of one of the younger girls. How would it feel to be coached by Ellie and her friends?

2. Ellie was feeling very frustrated with her setting skills. Getting a new perspective on those skills helped her see how to fix the problem. What is something that has made you feel frustrated? Write a two-page essay about your problem and how you solved it.

3. Ellie loves volleyball, even though she has to work hard to be good at it. Make a list of things you like to do that can be difficult.

MORE ABOUT
VOLLEYBALL

Volleyball was invented in Massachusetts in 1895 by William G. Morgan. Morgan was a friend of James Naismith, who had invented basketball four years earlier in Massachusetts.

Volleyball was first called "Mintonette." It was demonstrated at the Springfield, Massachusetts, YMCA by two teams of five male players. Soon after, the sport was renamed "volleyball."

In the earliest rules for the game of volleyball, teams could hit the ball around an unlimited number of times before hitting it over the net. Games were nine "innings" long, and each inning consisted of a team getting three serves.

Volleyball was introduced to the Philippines in 1910, and early games were played with a net strung between two trees. Filipinos are credited for coming up with the "three hits per side" rule. They also contributed to the three-hit strategy of bump, set, and spike.

The Olympics were held in Tokyo, Japan, in 1964. That was the first year that volleyball appeared as a medal sport in the Olympics.

Japan won the first women's team gold medal in Olympic volleyball. The U.S.S.R. won the first men's gold medal.